More Catholic Tales for Boys and Girls

More Catholic Tales for Boys and Girls

by Caryll Houselander

Illustrated by Renée George

SOPHIA INSTITUTE PRESS®
Manchester, New Hampshire

The stories in *More Catholic Tales for Boys and Girls* were originally published in *The Children's Messenger*, London, and were published by Sheed and Ward in 1956 in a single volume entitled *Inside the Ark and Other Stories*.

Printed in the United States of America

Cover design and illustration by Theodore Schluenderfritz

Sophia Institute Press®
Box 5284, Manchester, NH 03108
1-800-888-9344
www.sophiainstitute.com

Library of Congress Cataloging-in-Publication Data

Houselander, Caryll.
More Catholic tales for boys and girls / by Caryll Houselander ; illustrated by Renée George.
v. cm.
"The stories in More Catholic Tales for Boys and Girls were originally published in The Children's Messenger, London, and were published by Sheed and Ward in 1956 in a single volume entitled Inside the Ark and Other Stories."
Contents: Inside the ark — Bernard's pagan — The uncommunist cow — The donkey's legs — Montague runs away — The dancing bear — Loaves and little fishes — The Donkey-Boy's coat — Giving Mr. Oates — The white mouse's story — Anna Kluyer — Petook.
ISBN 1-928832-84-9 (pbk. : alk. paper)
1. Children's stories, English. 2. Christian life — Juvenile fiction. [1. Christian life—Fiction. 2. Short stories.] I. George, Renée, ill. II. Title.
PZ7.H8165Mo 2003
[Fic] — dc21 003002673

06 07 08 09 10 9 8 7 6 5 4 3

Contents

More Catholic Tales for Boys and Girls

Inside the Ark

Just before the strange and wonderful thing happened to us, I was dreaming a lot. I mean asleep-dreaming, not daydreaming. In my youth, I would have a fine, big dinner and sleep without moving, shut up, it seemed, in a tunnel of velvet darkness that had the evening star at one end and the rising sun at the other, and nothing at all in between. But as I grew older, I began to think that something had gone wrong with me or the world, or both. I would dream that I was hungry, and the hunger was gripping hold of my stomach like some great beast's teeth, a very nasty feeling. Or I would dream that I was fighting, my claws out, my eyes blazing, my body stiff, and my coat pricked up; and instead of doing it for fun and enjoying it, I was doing it in a rage and feeling ever so miserable.

I had a friend, a brontosaurus, very old and wise, and one day I went to see her and told her about my dreams and about the way life was all topsy-turvy. She listened with her eyes closed, nodding her great horned head and snuffling enormously now and then. Every time she snuffled, the whole jungle shook.

Well, after a time, she opened her eyes and said slowly, in a sing-song voice, as if she was inspired, "My friend Tiger, what you are coming to know is *sin*, alas!"

"Sin?" I said. "What is that?"

"It is hard for us animals to understand," she replied, "but as you know, I am some hundreds of years old, and I remember a time when no animal ever suffered at all. Things like hunger and thirst were pleasures; they only sharpened our joy in being alive. We used, even mighty beasts like myself, to pick our way on the grass not to tread down the opening flowers. We all knew that when we ate, we pushed our eager snouts into the invisible hand of a great Person. And that hand stroked and ruffled our fur and closed our eyes in sleep, and — "

The Brontosaurus broke off as if the memory was so lovely that she could not go on speaking of it. Then shaking herself and at the same time shaking all the neighboring bushes and the birds in them, she went on in a loud, violent voice: "Now all is changed. Man set himself up against God, against all the burning stars and flowing waters and springing fields, and he brought *our* troubles in the world. That's hard to understand. That's sin. And we animals feel it in our insides, in our dry tongues when we thirst, in our heaving flanks when we are hungry. Because of that, men, who used to love us and whom we used to serve, hunt us down, and we feel inclined, for our part, to eat them.

"Every sort of nasty thing happens now, and that, my friend, is why you dream. You, a tiger, get indigestion, and you dream! Alas!" She went on mumbling darkly, saying that sad things were gathering like a cloud of black flies, and no one knew where it would end, and so on, until she fell asleep. I slipped away, not really cheered up, to my own cave and my young wife, Mitsie.

It was to Mitsie that the call came first. She got up in the night and began pacing our cave, to and fro from wall to entrance, listening, listening. I rose with a thrilling shiver trembling through me and listened, too; but I heard nothing, at least only wolves howling, and nearer at home the squeak and scuffle of a mouse. Then Mitsie said, "Don't listen to outside. Listen to inside." So I did, and it was as if the sun had gotten inside us and called us. And now it led us out of the cave.

We trotted through the forest and were not surprised to find many other animals awake and trotting in the same direction. Their coats were all silvered in the moonlight, and they moved as if they were in a trance: tigers with little birds perching on their backs, and little silver mice scampering round their feet; bears and lions and zebras and rabbits and squirrels and weasels and every kind of beast, all together as friends, moving as if a gentle wind carried them along with it. You would not have supposed that any of these animals could quarrel and fight.

I remembered what the old Brontosaurus had said about everyone eating out of a big, kind hand. Now it seemed to me that this beautiful hand, although invisible, was stretched out over us all. As we turned out of the forest to the open plains, I saw many other animals coming from all the four corners of the earth: camels and elephants, and flights of birds like singing clouds, and on the ground hosts of shining insects.

As we moved on faster and faster, I saw that the wind was rising and the forests, now in the distance, were tossing and swaying like fields of grass. It was beginning to rain, too. I saw little diamonds glistening on our fur and hanging like dew on our whiskers. A feeling of hope and joy began to fill us, and we moved with a swinging movement, like dancing, like the birds that were circling overhead. We lurched from side to side and stamped our feet, and each in his own way, we started to sing. There was roaring and bellowing and squeaking such as I have not heard before or since.

And then I heard a new sound — a small sound, but so clear that it rang out more distinct and pure than all our singing put together. It was the sound of a man chanting.

Then I saw him: Father Noah, putting the last nail into the Ark that was already stirring, restively, like an impatient horse, on a rising lake of flood water. There he was, Father Noah, the first man I ever knew personally, the man who made me love men in spite of what they have done to us by bringing pain into the world with their sins. There he was, wearing a big leather apron and a broad sun hat, and he waved to us with his hammer in his brown hand and shouted a welcome.

It was crowded in the ark, and at first strange. Mrs. Noah was a homey soul and cooked some fine meals for us on her stove. Father Noah and his children brought them round to us twice a day. They brought us buckets of clean water, too, and armfuls of fresh straw and hay. We had stalls and bunk beds down each side of the ark. The small animals, rabbits and squirrels and the like, slept in the highest bunks, hogs and deer and so on in the middle bunks, and my own sort, tigers and lions, on the ground floor. In the middle of the ark, between our bunks, the Noah family lived. They had their table there and a small swinging lamp, and I always saw them, a little kind family, living in a ring of light, and all round them darkness; and out of that darkness the glowing eyes of beasts gazing, watching, wondering, questioning.

Outside the waters rose. Through the portholes we could see the black, swirling waters rising up as high as hills and dashing against the sides of the Ark higher and higher and higher, and the hard, sharp rain coming down into the water like hosts of sharp spears. We would have been afraid but for Father Noah. He was only a little man sitting there in his circle of light, but he made us feel safe, as if there were something about him that made him able to save us from all those strong, black towers of water, able to keep us safe and warm and fed in a world without forest, valley, or field, without cave or lair or nest or mountain rocks.

But at first I wondered how Father Noah could feel so safe himself, for even apart from the water filling the whole world, he had a great deal of worry. Even I could see that. First of all, he had all the food tubs to look after. Then there was all our straw to change, and the whole great Ark to sweep and scrub. And then there was keeping Mrs. Noah bright and happy, and looking after and teaching the three boys.

Poor Father Noah was the only man in the world, the only one who was good. He must have felt very lonely; at least I would have thought so.

I used to look at him and at all the glowering eyes of the watching beasts, shining out of the darkness on him, and one night I suddenly felt very much afraid for him.

I said to Mitsie, "Look how small Father Noah is. Do you know, Mitsie, if we liked, we could kill him: a blow from one of our great paws, a dart from a serpent's tongue — " I was going on, but Mitsie hushed me.

"Father Noah is greater than we are," she said, "although he looks smaller. For without him we wouldn't have any food or clean straw, and we would begin to fight and eat each other!"

"But how is it that he can be so strong and rule us when we are bigger than he is?"

"Listen," Mitsie answered, "you stay awake tonight and watch, and you'll know."

So I did. I saw the three Noah boys and their mother settle down in their rugs and fall asleep, and then Father Noah going softly around from bunk to bunk to see that all was well. I saw how tired he was, for his shoulders drooped and his eyes were heavy. I thought he would turn in when he had done his rounds. He looked at each beast, putting straight the donkey's blanket, patting the old camel, and giving the elephant a last bun. But when it was done, he didn't turn in at once. No, he blew out his lamp and knelt down, and he lifted his head toward the roof of the Ark as if there were someone there, and he began to speak.

"Lord," I heard him say, "You've destroyed almost everything that You made. There is no good grain growing on earth anymore, and no fish or fowl or flesh to eat. There are no flowers growing anymore to remind us of You, Lord, and nothing at all to lighten our load. It's hard work tending Your creatures and keeping them well and good. But, Lord, we've got one thing left, I know. We've got Your love. You are our Father, and we are in Your hands, and we won't perish."

Then it seemed as if a soft, warm light came all round Father Noah, and I saw the shadow of a great hand blessing him on the lime-washed ceiling of the Ark. So I knew Father Noah was safe, because he prayed, because he trusted in God.

About a week after this, the dove who had sat so patiently in the dovecote opposite me flew out at Father Noah's bidding and returned with a green olive branch. That was the sign that the waters were sinking, and the fields and the flowers and the forests coming again. Soon we were all going out of the open door into a new world, a green, shining world, washed pure and sweet and circled by a rainbow.

Bernard's Pagan

When Bernard read the story of Saint Francis Xavier, his heart took fire. He longed to go, as the saint went, into far-off lands, and with burning words and great sufferings, to save the souls of the pagans. He told this secretly to Father O'Leary, and Father O'Leary said, "You can't set out for the Indies yet, but you don't have to wait a day to start saving the souls of the pagans. It is three miles from your home to church; why don't you get up early in the morning and walk that three miles and receive Holy Communion for the poor pagans?"

"Well, I could," said Bernard, "but what about breakfast before school?"

"Take some bread and butter in your bag."

"Yes, I could, but how about hot tea?"

"Hot tea!" replied Father O'Leary. "If Saint Francis Xavier had bothered about hot tea, he wouldn't have saved a single pagan."

Bernard's mother smiled when he told her he was going to go to Mass every day before school, and his brothers laughed; for Bernard was not a boy who liked walking at all, or even playing games. He liked sitting in a chair reading, and he liked getting up at the very last minute before breakfast. They all laughed and said he could try, but he wouldn't do it for long. Bernard laughed, too, for he knew very well that he hated the idea of that walk every day. He wasn't at all the kind of boy who is very good at saying prayers anyhow, and it *was* funny to think of *him* saving the pagans. But it is well known that Saint Francis Xavier laughed a lot in his day, and maybe he did so when he set out on his long mission.

So Bernard began, and the road seemed very long, very dusty, and very dull. And each day it seemed longer, duller, and dustier. There were no shortcuts, no deep sweet fields to cross, no funny little lanes or twists to make it a nice sort of way. There were few landmarks to set off the stages of the journey and encourage him; but there was one, which stood by the roadside exactly halfway to church. This was a small, rather tumbledown cottage, a little way back in a patch of garden that was overgrown with weeds.

It was not a pretty cottage, but in a way it was friendly. Out of the crooked black chimney a thin line of smoke usually rose. The curtains over the smudgy windows were scarlet and cheerful, and on the door was written, "Abe Samson, Cobbler." It is difficult to imagine how Abe Samson, cobbler, made his living, for no one was ever seen to enter his gate with shoes to mend, and he was never seen to come out of his front door. Bernard often wondered what he was like. But although Bernard had never seen Abe, Abe had seen Bernard, and he was very curious indeed about him.

You may as well know at once that Abe Samson was a pagan. He dimly remembered the hot jungle in Africa, where he had been born. He could remember being a cabin boy on a ship years and years ago. He could remember being a sailor on another ship later on. He could remember being in all the great harbors of the world and all the distant cities. On his walls hung rugs from Persia, silver daggers from Turkey, spears and carved idols from Africa, horns and tusks engraved with wonderful patterns from India, silver bangles and heavy metal belts, skins of snakes and crocodiles, and many other treasures. On his floor there were the skins of tigers and the hoofs of elephants. All these things Abe had collected while wandering through the world in big ships, and about each of them he could tell a story.

But Abe had no one to tell his stories to. For while his heart was as gentle as a young lamb in April, his face was fierce and ugly. His nose had a gold ring in it. When he smiled, he showed a row of teeth like tusks. His eyes were large and sad, but when he talked, they glowed and rolled like the eyes of an ogre. And his hair was just a few grizzled curls.

Whenever he had come into port, Abe Samson had gone ashore and tried to find a child who would love him and listen to the stories he had to tell. But when he came toward them, they ran away and hid or burst out crying and screamed for their mothers. Then Abe would turn away and go back to his ship and wish he had a mother to write a letter to.

At last he came to England, with his treasures in big boxes and a bag of golden coins, and he bought his cottage. And because he had learned that people either laughed at him or were afraid of him, he stayed indoors all day and came out only at night.

Abe had never heard of God, except when sailors took His name in vain. But his heart was so tender that he had to worship something, so he worshiped the stars at night and his treasures by day, and sometimes his old pipe, because it comforted him, and likewise, for the same reason, his pot of tea brewing on the stove. Abe was not a cobbler, but when he bought his cottage, there was a board on the door with "James Samson, Cobbler" written on it; Abe liked the board, so he crossed out *James* and wrote *Abe*, and there you are!

Every morning Abe peeped through his scarlet curtain at Bernard and wondered where he went so early in the morning, for it couldn't be to school yet, or to go shopping.

Every morning when he got to Abe's cottage, Bernard took heart and remembered a thing Father O'Leary had said: "Never mind if you can't say much to our Lord when you get there, for every step of the way is an act of love." And indeed Bernard could *not* say much. He just knelt down and wondered why our Lord wanted so distracted and unholy a boy to come to Him every day, wanted it so much that He surely would save lots of pagans because Bernard came over three dull miles to please Him. And every day he grew more sure that our Lord *did* want him to come and would miss him if he failed. In the winter, it was harder; it was cold, and it was dark. Bernard had to count the steps that were acts of love as he walked them and say only how many they were when he got there.

But one thing cheered him every day: Abe's lamp in the window. And one thing cheered lonely old Abe: the sight of Bernard's eager face as he passed each day.

"I have sure guessed his secret," said Abe. "He is going to see someone he loves," and he chuckled behind the red curtain.

Then one day Abe looked the other way up the road, for he felt sure he would see the other person coming to meet Bernard, and he did. Someone was coming down the road and it was a Boy, too, a Boy who had about Him all the loveliness of all the children Abe had tried to love in all parts of the world. As the beautiful Boy came closer, Abe drew the curtain across the window, and his tears rolled down.

The next morning he looked out again, and again the Boy came. This time Abe started up with a cry, for the Child had His hands held out, and they were bleeding.

"Someone wounded Him," cried Abe and ran to his door, but he stopped with his hand on the latch and went back. "His friend will bind those wounds," he said, and all that day he sat, sad among his treasures.

Three days later, there came a knock on the cottage door. Abe had not looked out of his window for on that day he was ill. When he heard the knock, he sat up in bed, afraid, for it was the hour when the boys met outside his cottage, and he knew that one of them had knocked. In the stillness he heard his gentle heart beat, and the beating of it was like the fluttering of a poor dove in a cage, a dove that longed for all the sweet things outside and yet feared to go out to them.

Again came the knocking on the door, and Abe said, "Maybe it is the little one who has His hands hurt," and he forgot his ugly face, for he was afraid that the Child had no one to bathe His hands.

He got up and put on a dressing gown that had once been the robe of a Chinese mandarin. It was woven of green silk, and on it was a dragon of purple and gold and a rising sun. At the door was Bernard. Bernard raised his cap and smiled. He was very surprised, but not afraid. Anyone else would have been more surprised, but Bernard had been praying for pagans, and if this was not one, he would eat his hat. Being a polite boy, he did not say, "Are you a pagan?" but, "Good morning. Are you a cobbler?"

"Ah, yes," said Abe, "leastways, it says so on my door."

"Well, will you kindly mend my shoes?" and Bernard held out his shoes, soles upward, showing Abe the great holes that were the outward sign of all those steps that were the acts of love.

"Will you step in?" said Abe, who had no idea how to mend shoes. Bernard stepped in. He looked around, astonished, and he looked at Abe with his eyes shining, and Abe saw how this boy was delighted, and he laughed with joy.

"I can tell you stories of all those things," he said shyly, and he rolled up his green sleeve to show the tattooed things on his arms and added, "and of those things, too!"

Bernard longed to stay, but he shook his head. "Jesus is waiting," he said. "But tonight, when I pick up my shoes." And he went away wondering.

All that day Abe went about laughing to himself, and he hung Bernard's shoes up beside his bangles and kept looking at the worn patches and thinking of the other boy for whom they were worn into such great holes. "Must be Jesus," he said.

When Bernard came back, the shoes were still hanging on the wall, but Abe had a pair of sandals made out of plaited silver thread, and, grinning from ear to ear, he offered them to Bernard.

"It is very kind of you," Bernard stammered, "but, well, you know, I couldn't walk on the road in those nice sandals."

Abe rolled his eyes. "You could, too! Jesus does. You know He does when He comes down that long road to meet you!"

"When *He* comes? Mr. Samson, what do you mean?"

"What do *I* mean? Don't you know? Don't you go to meet Him?"

"Yes, but Mr. Samson, have you really *seen* Him? I thought you were a pagan."

So Abe told his story, and Bernard understood. He took Abe's big hand and told him about Jesus, and that He wouldn't run away, but was waiting for Abe to come and meet Him, too.

So it came about that Bernard had a comrade for half his way to Mass, for old Abe got out a top hat and a frock coat that he had come by in Paris and went to Father O'Leary. And soon he was going to Holy Communion every day with Bernard. And gradually his treasures disappeared.

One by one, they were taken down from the cottage wall and sent away to buy churches and schools far off over the deep waters Abe knew so well, and when the last glittering ornament was gone, the Child came to take the old man home.

The Uncommunist Cow

They were born in a stable and named Natasha and Tamara, twin sisters. It was not unfitting for *them* to be born in a stable (even such an old and poor one as this), for they were heifers — two long-legged red heifers, with dark violet eyes and big, soft ears. Poor though their stable was, it was always warm and cozy, for just as soon as a plank slipped from the roof or fell out of the wall, old Vassilly nailed it up again and never left more open than one little triangle in the wall. Through this the sisters could see a patch of sky: just a blue triangle, and a star that blazed like a diamond when the snow was down, but burned softly, like a golden candle flame in the green summer.

How lovely this stable was: the hay and straw so dry and sifted, always beaten up loose to lie on; the walls of pinewood, smelling sweet; always a good feed and a bucket of clean drinking water. In the daytime, Natasha and Tamara went out into the field, but there was a little mystery here. Old Vassilly never allowed the two to go out together. One was always shut in, while the other was out in the green grass and the sun. If the one who had to stay in began to moo even a little, to remind Vassilly that she was there, he would come in and scold her gently: "Hush, my darling, do not make a sound, or I will beat you with a stick!" He never did beat them with a stick, but it meant that mooing was dangerous.

Sometimes Vassilly brought a little boy into the stable with him. This was Mischa, his grandson. He was not unlike Tamara and Natasha in a way, for he had the same great, dark eyes, and, like them, he was very gentle and delicate in his movements. But while their hair was coarse and red-brown and all over them, his was all on his head, like fine silk, pale gold in color and cut square like the hair of an angel in a picture. The sisters could not help smiling when he stroked them, because his hands on their shaggy flanks were as cool and light as rose petals.

Mischa's father and mother had brought him to the old grandparents when he was a tiny baby. His father was a fine big soldier in the Red Army, and he said to old Vassilly, "You take him for us. I have to go and fight, and Vera here will work in the factory. The state would take him and put him in the orphanage, where he would have all sorts of things I never had, but he would not have a real little Russian home. Here he will have everything that makes it sweet to be alive in this darling world. And after this world, Heaven." So the young father and mother kissed the tiny Mischa, who was fast asleep, and went away with tears on their cheeks.

Vassilly's farm was only one field and a patch of vegetables, a few chickens and a cow, and a little low house with a living room and a kitchen.

Here Babooshka, as Mischa learned to call his granny, had a churn and made butter and cream. She also made loaves of black bread and sometimes, for very special feast days, little sweet cakes called *booblitchki*.

The walls of both rooms were whitewashed brick, and in the corner of the living room there was an icon of our Lady and the holy Child — that is, a very beautiful picture in bright colors and covered, except for the faces, with metal worked all over in flowers and tendrils and leaves and sheaves of corn and sheep and angels and holy words in Russian letters. In front of it a row of tiny green lamps was always burning. Green is the Russian's color for life, and Vassilly and Babooshka often went without other things in order to have the few pennies to buy oil for the lamps.

Now, it was forbidden for a farmer to have more than one cow, and Vassilly thought it wiser never to risk letting the twin heifers, who were exactly alike, be seen together, although there was not much fear of spies coming so far off the beaten track. All the same, Tamara and Natasha were never allowed to go out and play together in the green fields, as little sisters naturally want to do. This grieved them, for they dearly loved one another and hated being parted. If the one who was in the shed as much as mooed, old Vassilly would speak sternly to her. "Hush, my darling," he would say, "or I will have to beat you." But he never did, of course.

One day the unlikely thing happened. Mitya, a pale, nervous little government official, came by. He was leaning on the fence watching Tamara lying in the field, when he suddenly heard the sound of mooing from the shed. Mitya was not very clever. He had grown up without father or mother in a state orphanage, and no one had ever really been kind to him in his life. Since he had grown up and become an inspector of farms (because he had to), he had never done anything to please the government. He had never yet caught anyone breaking a law, and to tell you the truth, as he was very shy and very kind, he did not much want to. But he happened to have been badly scolded a day or two before, and he was feeling sore. So the soft mooing he could hear now in the shed would have seemed like Providence to him if he had believed in God. And, as it happens, it was Providence!

Walking stiffly to the shed, Mitya put on his fiercest face and strut, to make himself feel bolder, and flung open the door and found Natasha. He at once started shouting very loudly for the farmer to come out. This was fortunate, because it gave Vassilly warning, and while he ran out to answer the shouting, Babooshka hid the icon and the lamps.

"You know very well," declared Mitya, "that no one may have two cows. I shall have to arrest you."

At this, little Mischa, who had run out, too, began to cry, and Tamara and Natasha began to moo pitifully. Old Vassilly picked up his grandson to comfort him and hung his old white head down sadly over the golden one buried on his breast.

Mitya felt that he was being very rude and unkind and was ready to cry himself. He stopped shouting. "All right," he said in a shy, mumbling way. "I don't mean to be unkind, but one of your cows will have to be a Communist, and I shall take her away. I am really much above driving a cow across Russia myself, but I will not send someone else for her, for they would find a lot of things wrong here, I am sure. That little boy, now, he ought to be in a state nursery, where he would have everything, instead of this, this poverty." So Mitya cut a stick from a tree and started to drive Natasha away, while everyone on the little farm stood watching her go and seeing only a sad brown blur because their eyes were swimming with tears.

Poor Natasha arrived tired and frightened at a huge stable on a big Communist farm. A hundred other cows stood in a row, each in a painted stall. Into a hundred troughs food was poured

from a machine. The cows were milked by another machine. There was here no strong, human hand, no gentle human voice, no small child's kiss on the soft, expectant nose. Tears ran down Natasha's face, dark streams in her red hair.

"Whatever is wrong?" asked a cheerful, strapping young cow in the next stall.

"I want to go home," said Natasha.

"Home? What is home? I have always been told it's some sort of poor, dirty place where no cow is sure of her feed. Now, here you enjoy the worldwide sisterhood of cows, and you are sure of your regular food."

"A worldwide sisterhood isn't a bit the same as one darling little twin sister in your own sweet, warm home," sobbed Natasha. She ached for the dark shed and the burning star, the old man putting her patched rug over her, and the little child near her feet, and to press her flank against her sister's and smile into her violet eyes and smell her clover breath.

"You are a very unenlightened cow," said the Communist cow, and she shrugged her great shoulders and went to sleep. But Natasha could not sleep. She stayed awake thinking and thinking and thinking how to escape and go back home. Meanwhile, at home, little Mischa had fallen asleep praying for her to the Infant King who was born in a poor stable.

When Mitya was told, at noon on the following day, that his captured cow had vanished, he was afraid. Of course she would be on her way home, and someone would be sent for her. They would find out for certain all the wrong things he suspected, and perhaps he would be put into prison himself for not having told. "There is only one thing to do," he thought. "I must fetch her back myself."

During the night, snow had fallen, and it was easy enough to follow the print of Natasha's hoofs all the way back to her home. But it was a long way and took all the afternoon, and right into the late evening for Mitya to make the journey. Toward evening, it began to snow again, thicker and thicker and faster and faster; and when Mitya drew near to the farm and saw the glow of the fire in the kitchen window like a welcome in a world of cold white loneliness, he could not keep down a feeling of longing.

"At the moment of Mitya's arrival, the family were out in the cowshed, welcoming Natasha with tears and kisses of joy, all the more so because it was Christmas night, and it had looked as if it would be the saddest night they had ever known. Just as they were sitting down with heavy hearts to the Christmas feast, for which the old folks had toiled and scraped and saved for weeks, Natasha had come mooing (although weakly because of weariness) for joy to be home again. She had come straight to the kitchen door, and she had to be warmed and fed and made comfortable in the cow byre before they had their own meal.

So when Mitya opened the house door, no one was there. Yet he was greeted, really *greeted*, by a sight such as he had never seen before; the poor man's table laden with festive fare: a chicken, browned and sizzling in the dish, a bowl of white potatoes steaming by it, a new crisp loaf of home-baked bread, dishes of sugared fruits, *booblitchki* covered with white and pink icing, and in the middle of the table, a small Christmas tree, hung with bright little packages tied up in colored twine and fancy paper. Of course, the icon lamps were all filled with new oil and burning brightly with the green fire of life. And the table itself was lit by candles, so that the room seemed full of stars. The great stove was piled up with sweet-smelling logs, and the door of it was open, showing the bright flame and the blue smoke of the pinewood.

A sound of laughing voices woke Mitya from his trance as the family came back to the kitchen. They stood looking at him, and their eyes said, "What are you going to do?"

Mitya felt very miserable. "You know," he said, "I ought to arrest you."

Old Vassilly bowed. "Why, of course," he said, "but in the morning; for if you try to go out tonight you, as well as your prisoners, will perish in the snow. So stay with us tonight and share our Christmas. Tomorrow we will go where you wish."

Then, suddenly, old Babooshka started to laugh. "My poor little son," she said, "don't look so sad! Maybe you never saw a Christmas feast before. You had no home, no mother and father, but for tonight you belong to our family! Yes, for God is your Father, too, and the holy

Virgin is your mother, and the Child Jesus your little Brother. So sit down now, and make merry with us."

Then the fun began. Very soon Mitya was warmed up by Babooshka's homemade wine and the taste of such food as he had never dreamed of. He forgot all about tomorrow and joined in the laughter and the singing of carols, for little Mischa made him say the words after him. Then came the moment for the presents, and there was a lot of whispering and giggling between old Vassilly and Mischa, and at the end of it, Mischa handed one of his little packages to Mitya. In it was a painted cow, cut out of a piece of wood and colored by Vassilly.

"You see," laughed old Vassilly, "it was made only for a child."

"And *he* is a child," cried Babooshka, giving Mitya a hug and a kiss.

After the meal, they cleared away the table and danced in a ring, shouting and singing, until they were tired with joy. Then they stood in front of the icon to thank God for their Christmas day and the birth of His sweet Son. And Mitya stood there, too, with his head bowed and his heart full, although he knew no prayers to say.

In the morning, Vassilly took his hat and fetched Babooshka's shawl and Mischa's hood. "Now," he said, "since we are in God's hands, let us set out. We are your prisoners, Mitya."

"No, no, never!" cried Mitya. "May I not stay here and be a son to you and help you with your dear uncommunist cows?"

"But if they look for you?"

"They are not likely to find this place. I found it only by a rare chance. And if they do, well, as you said, old father, we are in God's hands. Now that I have seen a real home and know that the little family of God is so sweet, having all this for a short time will be better than a long life!"

"Of course!" cried Babooshka. "And you do not yet know all. After this life, we go to the real home. This is only a copy of it, as bad a copy as Mischa's funny drawing of a sunflower. And as you say, although we are out of men's sight here, God's eyes are always upon us, and His love always protects us. Here, son, take the pail and fill it with fresh water for Natasha and Tamara. And when you have done it, come back to listen, with your little brother Mischa, to the story of Christ's birth in a stable."

The Donkey's Legs

If you had gone walking in the narrow white lanes of the English countryside during the war, sooner or later you would have come upon Faroni's Traveling Fair. For even in wartime, the show was still carried on by Grandfather Faroni and the twins, and others who had lived and traveled with them for years and were now part of the family.

If you had come across the fair at nighttime, that would have added to the loveliness of it. You would have passed between hedges laden with hawthorn, through little hamlets sleeping in the darkness, past sweet-smelling fields of clover, and then suddenly you would have seen the fair, like a great ring of blazing jewels, all lit up with colored lights and glittering and jingling in the darkness. You would have seen and heard and smelled and tasted the fair!

There were the striped roofs of the stalls and the booths and the tents, all brilliantly colored; the merry-go-round, with its loud, jangling music repeating itself over and over again, and the little white horses with wide, red nostrils, the ostriches, crocodiles, and bears bobbing along to the music; the swing-boats, rushing up and down the night sky, crossing the stars. Then you would have heard the gusts of laughter, the loud cries of the showmen, the crack of the coconut-shies. And you would have caught the smell of hot canvas and of the earth cooling after the warmth of the sun on it all day. All that, and much more than that, is Faroni's Fair.

The twins were eleven. They did not know, themselves, exactly where the fair first began.

They had been to all sorts of countries with the fair: Spain, Portugal, Italy, Belgium, and many more, often crossing the sea in the lowest part of big ships, often being for days and days on the road. Wherever they went, they were welcomed, for they went only to little places off the beaten track, not to the towns, but to hamlets and villages. There, for a few pennies from each, they gave to people who had but little fun in their lives a *riot* of fun.

Ever since the twins could remember, they had been a sideshow in the fair. They had their special tent, and started as "The Live Water Babies," sitting in a tank of warm water, dressed in seaweeds and with little wreaths of shells on their heads. There were live goldfish in the tank, and the babies loved playing with them. In every country they had friends, children who played around the tents and loved to come and share a real gypsy meal with them. Grandfather had told them that wherever they went in the world, they would meet only their own brothers and sisters, because God is the Father of everyone. And it often seemed like that to the twins.

But then came the war, and all was changed: no more thrilling nights rocking in the great ships, no new countries. They stayed at home now, traveling in the summer and living dully in rooms in the winter. Then Father went away to fight, and next Mother, to make munitions, and after her Cora and Herman.

"I only wish I were younger," Grandfather said, "so that I could go, too, because the fighting is all to get peace again." He sighed and looked at the pink hawthorn and the blue sky over it.

"I wish *we* were *older,*" said Rupert, and Osbert, who always agreed with Rupert's ideas, nodded. They were thinking of their friends, brothers and sisters, whom they did not see anymore.

"We must all pray," said Grandfather, "and we should offer all we do for peace. And, however sad we feel, we can try to make other sad people laugh and forget their sorrows for an hour or so. That's war work, too."

That night Rupert touched Osbert's hand softly in the dark. "Say," he whispered, "wouldn't

Grandfather be pleased if we made up a really funny turn and did it as our prayer for peace?"

"Oh, yes," Osbert agreed. "Grandfather was saying today that all our jokes are worn out, and without Dad there is no 'go' in the show."

So they began to plot and whisper together for days on end, and finally they decided to be a dancing donkey.

They had an old pantomime donkey, with a large, doleful face, and they thought that nothing *could* be funnier than this beast dancing. So they got to work, and every time before practicing the dance, they prayed that all the world would learn how to love one another, and so peace would come and the end of the war.

But they could not agree which was to be the front and which the back legs of the donkey. "The front legs," said Rupert, "must be the shorter, and I am the shorter of us."

"No," Osbert answered, "the front legs are taller." Sometimes a fierce squabble set in, and sometimes they took it in turns, but at the end of each rehearsal, both boys said, "On opening night, I shall be the front legs."

At last the opening night came. Grandfather had proudly added "The Dancing Donkey" to the bill and posted a big picture of the donkey's face outside the tent. Soon the tent was filled and the people were waiting for the donkey to begin. In the excitement, Rupert forgot to hold out about being the front legs, and let Osbert slip into the skin without a word.

The donkey came slowly into the middle of the ring and bowed, and everyone clapped. Then the dance began: head on one side, tail flip, cross hoofs, and trip up! But no one laughed. The twins repeated the turn. Now and then a faint titter, but no laughter.

"Look here," whispered Rupert inside the donkey, "it's your fault. You're in my place. *I'm* the front legs."

"Rot," hissed back Osbert, and suddenly the donkey did the oddest thing. He kicked backward with his front legs!

"Ah, you *dare!*" said Rupert, and he lunged *his* leg forward. The front and back legs of the donkey were suddenly locked in a struggle.

At last the audience laughed. "Very clever," they shouted. "Bravo!"

But inside the donkey there was no laughing, only sharp, panting breath, gasps and sobs of fury: "You've spoiled it all!"

"Not me! *You* — *you've* gone and spoiled it!"

Wilder and wilder did the donkey's dance become. More and more strangely double-jointed, twisted, and elastic became the donkey. Louder and louder laughed the audience. Then suddenly the donkey rolled over in a heap, on the floor, while the audience screamed with delight.

"Time's up." The twins heard Grandfather's whisper — although they had not noticed the laughter of the people — and with tears streaming down their cheeks, they came out of the poor donkey to bow. Only then did they realize that everyone was shouting, stamping, and clapping for joy!

Outside the tent, Grandfather flung his arms around each twin in turn, beside himself with delight.

"My children," he cried, "you are actors! Artists, great artists! Superb actors! At first everyone thought, and even I thought, it was to be the usual thing that we have all seen a thousand times. But for a donkey to quarrel with himself! Ah! *That* was genius."

The twins crept away hand in hand, and sitting behind a tent, they talked it over. They were friends again now. Indeed, no quarrel of theirs ever lasted long. Rupert said, "Don't you think it's useless to pray for peace if even twins like us can't keep it?"

Osbert shook his head. "We could pray for God to make people more sensible than we are. But I've got an idea. Let's go on doing the donkey quarreling, only let's really do it on purpose!"

"Oh, yes! And that will remind us what donkeys we made of ourselves."

So the "Donkey's Dance" went on, and, most suitably, the twins felt like donkeys. The audience thought it was meant to show the world up as a bit of a donkey that has come to fighting with itself. But when Grandfather knew all about it, he was very pleased. "That's a real prayer for peace," he said, "a bit of penance for you and a real laugh for the people."

Montague Runs Away

About fifty years ago, the village of Looming was a dull place to live in. Nowadays people who love old things and places go there and stare at the gray stone cottages and the cobbled streets and the little blue and pink flowers that grow in the chinks of the walls. And, nowadays, you can go there in a car, which was not the case when Montague lived there, fifty years ago, with Aunt Priscilla. For in those days, no one had a car, and although some people had bicycles, Aunt Priscilla did not. Although she was quite young and even, sometimes, quite sporting, she did not think bicycles ladylike and therefore would not ride them. There was no train station at Looming then, and for that matter, there is not one now; but of course, in those days, you could go away only in a carriage or a cart, which meant that you hardly ever went away.

Montague was the apple of his aunt's eye, but in those days, being the apple of someone's eye was not much fun. It usually meant that they were very anxious about you, and therefore very strict with you. Aunt Priscilla was very strict indeed. She was always asking Montague if he had brushed his teeth, learned his lessons, and said his prayers.

So, except for two weeks in the year, Montague was bored. One week was the week when the circus came; the other was the week of the mission. In the ordinary way, the sermons in church were rather dull, but the mission sermons were generally exciting. This year a different sort of missionary came. He said some things about sins and about Hell, but he spoke more about how to love God. He told stories of men who had gone, in olden days, to distant countries for the love of

God, to bring Christ to those far-off people — men such as Francis Xavier and others who had lived in little villages like Looming, with the peaceful hills around them and the sound of church bells ringing in their ears, but who, for the love of God, had gone far away in ships to other lands, to people who worshiped idols. And he told of the things that happened to the missionaries: of their adventures, how they fell into the hands of pirates and of savages, and very often in the end laid down their lives for God.

The missionary's words burned into Montague's heart. He began to imagine himself going with a sword in one hand and the Gospel in the other, to cross the foaming seas and discover new lands. Only, Francis Xavier had no sword! Well, he, Montague, could have a secret invisible sword of love, and he would have great adventures for God, and he would never feel dull anymore.

A week after the mission had gone, the circus came, and Aunt Priscilla said, "What a good thing we have just had the mission, to prepare us for the excitement and save us from being carried off our feet!"

"But I may go to the circus, may I not?" said Montague.

"Well, we shall see. If you are very good." Montague knew he would go, but every day the circus would be used as a threat and a bribe about goodness. In the meantime, he could go out and look at the posters. "Cottelengo's Circus" in flaming letters lit up the twisting gray street, and there were pictures of elephants and tigers.

"Now mind," said Aunt Priscilla when they saw them, "mind to change your shoes when you come in, or you will catch a cold and be unable to go." But Montague saw the pink flush in Aunt Priscilla's cheeks, and he knew that she, too, longed to go.

It was the day before the circus started that Montague saw José Cottelengo for the first time. He had come out to look at the bright caravans camped in the fields between Looming and the sea. He knew it was rude to stare, even at funny people, but he felt sure that Francis Xavier must have stared sometimes. And so, although the circus people were polite and took no notice of him at all, he stood as near as he dared go and stared hard.

Among the gypsies, José stood out sharp and beautiful and heathen. He was dark-skinned, with thick black hair and long, sleepy-looking eyes. He might have been a year older than Montague, but was thinner and taller and broader, with strong brown hands and bare legs and feet.

Montague told Aunt Priscilla, but she was furious. "You must keep away from them," she said. "They may be very wicked. Those circus people are said to lie and steal, and their language is such that no one could hear it without blushing."

Then the flame leaped up in Montague. The call had come. If José Cottelengo was wicked, if the circus, with its bells and its drums and its tinsel and scarlet, was a pagan land moving on wheels through the world, he would be a missionary called to convert the circus.

On the night of the circus, Montague was not sure whether he felt good or wicked as he put on his galoshes. He knew that within a few hours, he would kick them off, and his shoes and stockings also, and run on the grass with bare feet. And the idea of being a priest was gradually — no, suddenly — changing to the idea of being a clown. After all, he could be a very apostolic kind of clown! He was not quite as happy as he had hoped to be when he sat by Aunt Priscilla's side and watched it all. He kept looking at her out of the corner of his eye. She sat very straight, wearing her feather boa and her lavender gloves, and laughed moderately, in a ladylike way, at the clowns. When the trapeze act came on, she shut her eyes, and when the lions appeared, she sniffed her smelling salts. "I wonder if she'll be lonely," thought Montague, but he put aside the thought. After all, Francis Xavier never wondered if his aunt would be lonely.

All the same, he felt awful when he got up early next morning and slipped out of the house without his overcoat or galoshes and without his shoes or stockings. But he was down the street and out toward the field in a minute. And then he forgot everything: Aunt Priscilla and his mission and everything except the circus and the wonderful life of the drums and the scarlet and the cracking of whips.

He had a few miles to go before he caught up with the caravans. When he reached them, he did not quite know what to do next, so he kept a little way behind. He could hear the sound of the circus people's voices and laughter inside the caravans, and at first it was lovely to follow them along the country roads full of the smell of the hedges. When the vans stopped, he got over the hedge and ate the buns he had brought with him. Then the caravans went on, and Montague followed again.

Presently he found that he was tired and rather cold and had blisters on his heels, and he was frightened. He couldn't walk anymore. What could he do?

In a panic, he knocked on the door of the nearest caravan. There was a pause in the laughter, and then, with jerkings and rumblings, the caravan stopped. Inside, it was very hot and smelled of garlic. There seemed to be a lot of people, a ring of dark, smiling faces all around him, a lot of white teeth and golden earrings. A very large woman with a very tiny baby on her arm was talking to him, but he did not answer her questions.

He was much more tired than he knew, and in the heat, he grew more and more sleepy. He wanted Aunt Priscilla, but he could not stay awake, and the kind big woman with the baby picked him up and put him in one of the bunks.

When he awoke, it was afternoon. The van was halted and was empty of all but José, who was standing, staring at him.

"Want to wash?" José said.

"Yes."

"All right. Come to the stream."

Montague followed him, and the stream was cold and lovely.

"Go on," said José. "Put your head in. That isn't washing. That's dabbling." So he put his head in and choked and spluttered, but felt better afterward. "What are you going to do now?" asked José, grinning.

Montague thought, "I mustn't be a coward. I've got to say *something*." So he said, "Could I stay with you and be a clown?"

José shook his head. "Clowns are born," he said.

"Well, I'm born."

"Ah, but you weren't born a clown."

"Were *you* born a clown?"

"No. I am born to tame lions."

Montague looked at him with wonder. "How awful!" he said.

José shrugged his shoulders. "Not if you're born for it. But I'd rather be a missionary."

"What!" Montague sat bolt upright and stared.

"I'd rather be a missionary," repeated José. "That's not funny. You see, I've seen the towns when we go through. The people there don't know God, not as we do. They don't see the stars and the flowers and the water, not the way we do, and they don't know that God's beautiful."

José leaned forward and clasped his knees with his hands, and his dark face frowned as if he were desperate to explain what could not be explained.

"You see, it's like this," he went on. "They know how there is a God, and they know how He gets angry if they do wrong. But they don't know what God's like one bit. They don't know how He loves funny things. Why, if you'd seen some of the little frogs and field mice and spiders that I've seen, you'd know God likes to laugh, or else He wouldn't make those things. Of course, He's serious, too, and He makes stars shine right down in the wells and the streams. And then there's the way He does things. I've seen the fields all the year round; I've seen 'em when the seed goes in and when it starts to come up, and when it's all shining like gold for the harvest." He stopped as if he felt he couldn't explain any more.

Montague, staring at him, saw that around his neck was a silver medal. "Are you a Catholic?" he whispered.

"Yes. We come from Italy. At least our grandfather did. But look here, what did you come after us for?"

Then, rather shamefacedly, Montague told his story.

At the end, José said, "Well, it was very mean and silly of you. And I'll bet that Saint Francis Xavier would have told his aunt what he wanted to do. But it's all right. My brother Jake went back as soon as you were asleep to fetch your aunt. You've got your name on your clothes, you see. I should think she'll spank you. Anyway, you can't be a missionary just yet."

"But José, why don't *you* be a missionary, instead of putting your head into a lion's mouth?"

"I haven't any learning," said José, "or any books. Missionaries have to know a lot of things. They've got to know Latin and be priests so they can give people our Lord. Else they can't do much. I couldn't tell people about God, only about the things I've seen Him doing and how He laughs and how He wants us all to be happy."

* * *

Aunt Priscilla was always a surprising person.

She arrived on a bicycle, and without gloves, and instead of spanking Montague, she kissed him. And when she found it was impossible to get home, two of them on the same bicycle, before dark, she agreed to stay in the caravan for the night. She didn't undress, of course, but did like perfect ladies do on a Channel crossing: she put up her feet, tilted her hat over her eyes, and dabbed her forehead with scent.

When they were at home again, she had the biggest surprise for Montague. "I'm going to buy a caravan," she said, "and we are going to follow the circus in the summer and have a little school for them. I shall teach. Don't interrupt, please. You were naughty to run away, but I was naughty to think circus people wicked just because they are circus people. So I'm going to forgive you, and God will forgive me. We both owe José a school, so we'll give him that. And *won't* it be fun? Now don't say a word, Montague, but go and wash your face for tea. You look a sight!"

The Dancing Bear

Every year the dancing bear came to the village. The old peasant women said that if you had a tummy ache and the bear danced on your tummy, it would never ache again, but nobody tried it to see. Everyone loved the bear. He was brown and shaggy and loved children. You could pat and stroke him, and you could see that he was pleased when the children clapped at his dancing.

Nickie longed for the bear more than ever this year, because Father had promised that he would come to his Christmas party and dance inside the big hall. That would be something no other child had ever had. Nickie always had what he wanted when they came to the country house, but in the town he did not, for he was a prince and he had to work hard, learning lots of languages and doing lots of drill. He had tutors for everything: one for sums, one for manners, another for French, and so on. He was only allowed to play with boys who were the sons of noblemen or important soldiers, and altogether life in the town was very boring.

He often said, "I hate being a prince." All the same, if anyone told him he could not do something he wanted to, he would stamp and shout and tell them to remember that he was a prince. It was as if two people lived in him: one who wanted to rule and have everything and another who wanted only to play with the village children and have fun. But the village children were shy of him, and because he came to the country in the first automobile they had ever seen, they thought he was magic and ran away and hid. They did not come to his parties, but sometimes Father gave special parties for them and Nickie went around giving each a present. They took the presents shyly, but stared at him and only whispered their thank-yous.

Nickie's birthday was Christmas day, and this year he would be nine. His cousins would come to stay, and there would be the wonderful party with the bear. "When the bear man reaches the village," Father had told a servant, "go and tell him that it is the prince's birthday, and so he must bring in the bear to dance to him."

The day had come now. It began with the Liturgy in the village church, and Nickie was rather bored, the service was so long. He kept still and stood stiff and straight and sometimes bowed his head to the ground, but his thoughts kept flying to the dancing bear that would come in the afternoon.

The tables were spread and the lamps were lit, and on the tables, among the tall, white sugar cakes and the great red candles, were piles of crackers and preserved fruits. All the guests had arrived, and now it was time for the bear to come. Nickie could hardly wait. Everyone stared toward the door, expecting that at any moment the old man would lead the bear in. Father paced up and down and kept looking at his watch. But the bear did not come. "Did you tell the old man what I said?" he asked the servant.

"But yes, exactly," he answered. "And the old man was so pleased. He said that never before had such an honor come to his poor beast, and his eyes filled with tears of joy."

"Then it is strange he does not come," said Father. Nickie began to be afraid that something had happened to him and he would not come at all.

"Well, let's eat," suggested Nickie's greediest cousin, "and perhaps he'll come after."

"No, I can't eat," said Nickie. "I *must* have the bear." He thought of praying that the bear would come; but he got very uneasy and red-faced, because he remembered that he had really not said any prayers at the Liturgy, even though this was Christ's birthday, too. He looked at the icon of the Christ Child in the corner, a grave, oval-faced Boy behind a green light, very dark in His big, gold halo. For the first time, Nickie thought, "How lonely Christ looks in His stiff gold coat." Then suddenly he forgot the bear and said to his Father, "Look here, I forgot to wish a happy birthday to Christ. I want to go to church and do it now."

"But now you must entertain your guests."

Nickie set his mouth into a stiff line. "First," he said, "I must wish Christ a happy birthday."

And so, because he usually had his own way in the country, and this was Christmas Day, Nickie dressed in his fur coat and cap and set out in his sledge over the snow. It was a short way, a lovely white drive between trees that bore crystals for berries. "I shall go in alone," said Nickie when they got to the church, and he walked up the path by himself and pushed open the door.

There, instead of the empty, dark church lit only by the tiny flames before the icons, was a place full of warm, glowing light and ringing with the sound of laughter and clapping! The children of the village were gathered in a circle all round the big icon of the Nativity, and in the middle of the circle, the shaggy brown bear was dancing to the Christ Child. There was a look of wonderful pride and joy on the bear's face, as if he understood. He stamped to and fro from one padded black foot to the other, panting and grunting with delight. And the old bear man stood by with tears in his eyes, his lips moving in prayer.

Nickie stood behind them all. He knew what had happened. When the servant gave the old man Father's message, he had thought it meant Christ's birthday, for who is "the Prince" but Christ? And Nickie could not tell the holy man that it was only he who had wanted the bear. He could not see all the joy spoiled. Besides, Christ, who had seemed so lonely, must be joyful now, with all the peasant children laughing around Him, and the poor beasts and the holy old man at His party.

So the little prince stood and prayed for the grace to be brave, and when the dance was over, he clapped with the others and patted the bear. He would have liked to have given a gold coin to the old man, but he did not, because he knew that no one can pay for service done to God. And now that he, too, had given Jesus a birthday present, he knew what joy giving to Him can be.

But he asked everyone to come and share his birthday tea: the bear man, the villagers, and the bear. Only he said nothing about dancing and asked the others not to. That was the loveliest Christmas party Nickie had ever known, and the peasants, too, and, for that matter, the sweet-toothed, shaggy old bear.

Loaves and Little Fishes

During the minnow season at the Round Pond, there are so many minnow fishers that, if there were more, a good number would have no room to put their nets into the pond. Yet on a certain Saturday evening at five o'clock, only one remained, and he sat with his net dangling limply in the water, and a face of woe.

Tommy Richards had had a bitterly disappointing season: three Saturdays of fishing and not a catch! It was an *almost* unheard-of thing for anyone, *quite* unheard of for Tommy. He was the best fisherman in his street. He had come home day after day the summer before with a full jam jar, so full that in the sun it looked like a silver jar. And besides being the envy and admiration of the whole street, Tommy had carried on a fair trade, for after the actual catching of them comes the exchange and sale of minnows. And while this lasts, it takes up the whole of everybody's spare time.

It is ordinary to exchange your largest or smallest minnow for one of exactly the same size and brightness, since it is not for mere gain that the trade exists (although, as a matter of fact, there are sales; about two dozen fish go for five cents). But the real reason for the trading is one you cannot fail to see: simply that it is fun to exchange minnows.

The thing that really hurt Tommy was that every night now, when he went home with his empty jar, the boys laughed at him. Tommy must have boasted and been a little stuck-up the year before, as generally boys are sorry for anyone with an empty net; but these boys laughed and made up jeering little rhymes to sing when Tommy came down the street.

"Tonight," Tommy had said to that unpleasant boy, Ginger, "I won't come home until I *have* caught something." And, of course, he knew that Ginger would tell all the others that rash remark. So there he sat, his net dragging in the water, the sorriest fisherman that ever sat by the Round Pond.

While he sat there, Rupert Agar was wheeled up in his wheelchair and sat gazing at the great silver circle of water with dark, sad eyes. Rupert was a very thin, very white, very silent boy. Tommy had often seen him before, but this was the first time he had been alone with him. (Rupert's nurse sat on a bench just far enough off not to hear if they talked.) He was not the kind of boy Tommy liked. He was Jewish, and Tommy was one of those foolish people who have likes and dislikes simply because all the other people they know have the same.

But today Rupert was more interesting than usual, and Tommy was more ready to be nice to anyone who would be nice to him than he had ever been before. Rupert was more interesting today because for the first time in his life, he had brought a net and now was casting it into the water. (A minnow net is exactly like a butterfly net.) Tommy drew near.

"Got a jar?" Tommy said, as an opening to friendship.

Rupert smiled. "The nurse has the bottle," he replied.

"What did you give for that net?" said Tommy.

"Ten cents."

"It's a pretty good net for ten cents!"

Rupert smiled again. It made him look much nicer. "I do hope I get something," he said.

"Yes," said Tommy with feeling. "It is hard to go home empty-handed." And just as he said that, he felt a wriggle in his net. It was a minnow — just one, smaller than half of your little finger, but a minnow that would save his honor after all!

He put it in his jar and cast in his net again. He crossed his knees and began to whistle. He thought the day had gotten warmer all of a sudden, and he began to want his supper. Also, he felt more kindly than ever toward Rupert. "Where do you live?" he said.

"Harley Street," said Rupert.

"What do you do? Go to school?"

"No, I'm ill. I just be ill, that's all."

"I'd like to be ill," said Tommy.

"Why, it's no fun. Why do you want to be ill?"

"To go to the hospital and see God."

"Oh, you wouldn't see God. You'd see the doctor."

But Tommy insisted. "A fellow I know got ill, and he went to the hospital and saw a man bring God to another ill boy there. He told me so!"

"Well, I don't believe it," said Rupert, "but what did God look like?"

Tommy didn't want to say like a round white thing (that is what the fellow had said). He thought Rupert would not be thrilled, so he thought hard and then said, "Like a very big man made of satin, with a big pointed hat on, and a gold crook in his hand and gloves on with a ring outside." Tommy felt uncomfortable saying this, because he knew very well that it was the bishop he was describing; but as he thought the bishop was the most wonderful thing he had ever seen, he pretended that that was what God looked like.

Rupert *was* thrilled, so much so that Tommy felt he must tell him that he had seen something very like God with his own eyes. So he told him about the time when he really had seen the bishop, once when he went into a church to keep dry on a very wet day.

"He was dressed up just like God," he said, "and I think he was a relation of His, he was so like Him. And he was smoking, and the smoke smelled lovely, not like chimney smoke at all, not smoking a pipe, but smoking as if he were on fire but didn't get burned."

Tommy really had thought it was God, but he had heard one of the people coming out say it was the bishop. All the same, Tommy thought, he must be connected with God, for everyone fell on their knees when he walked down the church at the end.

So Rupert and Tommy talked and told one another a lot of things and began to like each other very much. Presently Rupert's nurse came up and said they must go. Then it was that Rupert did something that shocked Tommy: he began to cry, really hard, crying like a baby, although he must have been as old as Tommy, about nine years old.

"I haven't got a minnow," wailed Rupert. "I haven't got a minnow."

The nurse tried to comfort him in vain. Tomorrow he might get one. Tomorrow was no good; he wanted one today. He cried and cried, and the poor nurse looked quite afraid. "It makes him very ill to cry," she said to Tommy.

Then Tommy did a very big thing, a thing that made a big difference to the whole of his life: he took his minnow, jam-jar and all, and put it into Rupert's hands. "There you are, cry-baby," he said and walked away quickly, in case he might snatch it back.

The next day, when Tommy, not alone this time, but with Ginger and the other boys, sat fishing, Rupert came again. For Tommy it had been a bad evening; he had gone home empty-handed and found Ginger and his followers lined up with their hands held out, asking for a fish. He had held up his head and walked past, but it was a terrible moment.

Today when he saw Rupert coming, he went very red. He knew that all the boys would laugh at him if he spoke to him, and he hated to be laughed at. But Tommy was a gentleman, and he knew very well that you don't pretend not to know a person to whom you have given a minnow. So he went boldly to meet Rupert and sat down beside him. The sad little boy was delighted.

"My fish is still alive," he said, and they talked. Tommy shouted in fact, to drown out the mean things Ginger was saying close by.

And so it went on day after day, until the end of the fishing season. And on the last day, Rupert came, not in his wheelchair, but walking. It had been a very hard time for Tommy. Ginger was the leader of the boys now, and he had not spared his rival. It had meant more than one fight and Tommy had come off badly in the fighting. He was glad, then, when Rupert told him that now that he was better, he was going away to school. He liked Rupert; in fact, he liked him very much.

But he liked being liked by the other boys still more, so he was glad to say good-bye.

During the winter, Tommy got his wish: he went to the hospital. First of all, he became a baker's boy and took the bread around every morning. Then he got run over and went to the hospital. For the first few days, it wasn't very nice; in fact, it was very unpleasant indeed and he began to wish it hadn't happened after all. Then the hurting part was over, and it got to be very nice. People he didn't know brought him candy and books to read. He had wonderful meals and made a new friend in the doctor. But he did not see God. Every time a stranger came into the room, he looked to see if he was bringing God, but he was always disappointed.

All the same, he saw someone else very exciting: the bishop's cook. Her little boy was ill, too, and she came to see him and talked to Tommy as well. She was a very special person indeed; she had a very gentle way of talking and told most wonderful stories. Best of all, she loved talking about the bishop. She told Tommy that he was very near to God, and when Tommy asked her if God really was a little round white thing, she explained that the bishop was able to turn a white host, which was bread, into God.

From that time, Tommy longed to see the bishop again and to ask him to give him this bread that was God. And he had great hope, because the kind cook promised that he would leave loaves at the bishop's house every morning when he got well again.

Before he did get well, another thing happened. There was a party in the hospital, and Rupert came to it and brought his father with him. Of course, he was very surprised to see Tommy again and introduced him to his father. His father was a very odd man, Tommy thought. He wanted to pay Tommy for the minnow he had given to his son. Since Tommy was a gentleman, he naturally felt angry at anyone wanting to pay for a gift; and then Rupert's father wanted to pay such a *lot*. Tommy knew very well that it is not right to let someone pay a huge sum of money for something worth less than a penny. What that fish had cost him in shame and fighting (both with himself and Ginger) was something that Rupert's father could never understand. Tommy knew that that could be paid, if at all, only in some other way. So he scowled and said, "No."

It did not surprise him to know that Rupert had begun getting better from the day he had had the minnow, because he remembered how well he had felt himself when he saw it wriggle in his net, and how bad he had felt when he had given it away.

When he got better, Tommy left five small loaves every day at the bishop's house, and every day he asked the soft-voiced cook when he would see the bishop. But every day she shook her head and said that the bishop was very ill. He had not been run over like his baker's boy, but he had gotten very ill through having a lot to worry over when he was so old. And every day Tommy got more and more afraid that the bishop would die before he would be able to see him and ask him for this bread that was God.

Then one day a wonderful idea came into his head: if one minnow had cured Rupert, surely several would cure even the bishop. They might even make him young again and able to worry without being ill. So one morning Tommy arrived at the house with a jam-jar hidden under his loaves, and in it were two minnows. He had hoped for more, but two were all he had caught. He knew the cook would never let him go to the bishop's room, and he was afraid she wouldn't give him the fish either. It was a thing she did not understand, that minnows made people well. She had faith in fried soles, but none in living minnows. So Tommy had to do something terribly daring and terribly frightening. He had to wait until the cook was not in the kitchen and slip in at the back door, still carrying his basket.

Holding his breath, he crept through the kitchen into the hall. He felt sure the bishop's room was upstairs, so with a trembling heart he crept up. On the landing he put down the basket and sniffed; he sniffed because he knew the bishop smelled of the wonderful blue smoke he had seen coming out of him, but he sniffed in vain. So, more and more afraid (for to him there was something frightening about the bishop), he opened a door and slipped into a big, silent room.

The bishop was not there — or was he? There was an old man in bed propped up against the pillows. But he had no silk clothes and no long pointed hat; he wasn't smoking; he was not even frightening, and yet he had the bishop's face! He was propped up on the pillows, looking very small. And he was doing sums. There were pieces of paper with sums on them lying about on the bed. Tommy knew at once why he was worried; sums worried him, too. And it looked to him as if the bishop couldn't do his. He was frowning and biting the end of the pencil, and the papers had bits all over it that he had scratched out.

But strangest of all, sitting on a chair beside him was Rupert's father!

When Tommy came in, the bishop dropped the pencil and jumped. Rupert's father jumped, too, and said, "Well, I am blowed," in such a loud voice that Tommy did not hear what the bishop said himself. Tommy suddenly felt so shy that he couldn't say a word. He stood still holding his basket, his mouth open for words to come out, and none came. Then Rupert's father took his basket from him and looked in it.

"Well, I am jiggered!" he said, and he certainly *looked* blowed and jiggered. "The boy has two little fishes and a lot of loaves!" he exclaimed, and he shook Tommy's hand so furiously that he nearly squealed.

"How many loaves?" said the bishop in a very sweet voice, rather like his cook's.

"Five," said Rupert's father; and suddenly the worried bishop smiled, and held out his hand. Tommy felt unshy when the bishop smiled, and he went up to him with the jar.

"I brought them to make you well," he said, and they must have made the bishop well, for he took the jar into his hands and began to laugh. And Rupert's father sat down and laughed, too, very loudly, stamping on the floor and slapping his knees, not at all as a person behaves with an ill person. And when the bishop had laughed a lot, he wiped his eyes on a silk handkerchief and said, in a still-laughing voice, "Dear me, dear me! How these minnows do take me back. Why, I feel about ten years old again!"

Tommy rejoiced. "I knew it!" he said. "I knew it. I knew they would make you well and young so that you could worry without minding and getting ill!"

Then Tommy told the bishop the whole story. Rupert's father put in bits, too, and explained how his son had gotten well, and he had told Tommy it was because he gave him a fish.

"And why did you want me to get well?" said the bishop.

"Because," Tommy told him, "because I want you to make bread into God so that I can have Him very near me, like He is to you."

Rupert's father was always doing odd things; now he did a very funny one: he took the bishop's sums and tore them up, and said, "Look here, you shall do a bit of addition instead."

"I would rather multiply," said the bishop in his gentle voice, and he touched the loaves as if he loved them.

"I am going to tell you something," Rupert's father said. "I made the bishop do sums, and they made him ill." (Tommy knew that.) "He has a school, and he pays me the rent, and I was going to give it to someone else who pays more, and now" — he paused and looked at the bishop while he spoke — "and now, if you will let me, I am going to pay for Rupert's minnow after all. I am going to give you the school in exchange for it, and if you like, you can let the bishop use it."

That is the whole story of Tommy's minnow. The bishop got quite well, and he gave Tommy the Living Bread, and Tommy gave him the school; but he lives in the bishop's house and goes to the school himself. He still keeps all his old friends, and Ginger has learned to respect him, and Rupert goes with him to the Round Pond on his holidays, and they catch their fish together. The bishop helps Tommy to do his sums, and they both like multiplication.

The Donkey-Boy's Coat

Joey and Beckie were friends, although Joey was a boy and Beckie a donkey. In fact, Joey was the donkey's stable boy. Every day he groomed her, brushed her down, combed out her tail and polished her hoofs. He also fed her every morning and evening, stirring her mash carefully and taking it to her nice and warm, and drawing up a bucket of cold, clean water out of the well for her to drink. And although Joey was poorer than the donkey (who belonged to a rich man), he often took something for her from his own dinner plate, a carrot or a lump of sugar.

Beckie loved Joey in her turn. She rubbed her soft nose against his cheek to say so, and let him fondle her lovely colt from the hour it was born. She was so proud of her colt that it quite astonished Joey to see the look in her eyes when she gazed on it. Beckie and her colt each had a rug of warm dyed wool, woven in stripes of red and purple and orange; but Joey had only a comic-looking coat that made other boys laugh. It had come down from three older brothers, patched and threadbare, and was still a bit too big for Joey. And its once-beautiful pattern was nearly all washed out of it.

Joey lived in Palestine at the same time as our Blessed Lord. His three older brothers were always talking about the Prophet Jesus of Nazareth and what He would do for them. For they had seen Him, and once or twice had heard Him preach to the people. These were the sort of things they said to one another when they talked about "the Prophet Jesus," for they did not yet understand who He was, or what He had come to do for men.

"He will set Israel free," one would say.

"We Jews will soon rule over the Romans," the next would cry. "I shall be among the first of His soldiers, and He will make me captain of His army."

"I shall be His prime minister."

"We will all be rich and powerful. We'll own our own fields and vineyards."

"And you, youngster," they would add, turning to Joey, "what are you going to ask Him to do for you, when He comes into His kingdom?"

"Nothing," said Joey.

"Nothing!" There was a shout of laughter at this. "Just hear our lunatic brother!" they cried.

"Well, I *saw* Him once," said Joey, "and ever since, I've wanted to do something *for Him;* but not so I would be great. But there is *one* thing — "

"Out with it!" cried his brothers.

"I wish," said Joey slowly, "that He would do something nice for Beckie's colt. It would please Beckie so."

There was another burst of laughter at this, and Joey, rather red in the face, went off to the stable. As he came close to the stable, he was surprised to see the door open, and inside were two men undoing the colt. "Why are you untying the colt?" Joey said.

They turned very kind, good faces to him, and Joey liked them at once. "It is because the Lord has need of it," they said.

The Lord!

Joey knew whom they meant: Jesus of Nazareth. He watched them leading Beckie and the colt away, and he thought, "I ought to go, too." Then he remembered his shabby coat, with the pattern all worn off, and he felt too shy to go near the Lord in it. But the donkeys were in his charge, and so he ought to be with them. He kept saying, "Yes, I'll go," then no, then yes, and at last he ran after the men and the donkeys.

He ran down the road by which they had gone. They had disappeared around the bend, but when they came in sight again, there was Someone else with them. Joey stopped short. He caught his breath, and his heart beat fast. He knew that it was the Lord. The two men were laying their coats on the colt's back. No one had ever ridden on the colt before, but Joey guessed that the Lord was going to ride him now. Yes! He saw Him get onto the colt's back, and set off slowly with His companions following Him.

And then, from all the hamlet around, just as if a secret message had come to them (as it comes to birds, telling them to rise in flocks and fly to sunny lands) children, crowds of them, came into sight. They were all running toward the gates of the city of Jerusalem. First, there were little groups of them; then big groups, as they joined up; then a great crowd. And as they ran, they leaped up and down and waved green branches gathered from the trees.

Joey ran with them. It was like a little running forest! The whole multitude carried long, green palms and kept crying out "Hosanna!" At the gates of the city they halted. Then the Lord came, riding on the colt. Joey forgot his poor coat, its shabbiness and absurdness, and when he saw the children throwing down their garments under the colt's feet, he threw his patched coat down, too. When the Lord had passed into the town, Joey picked up his coat and put it on again. He gave no thought to it. He was walking as if in a dream. Joy was rising in his heart as he pushed his way through the gates, following the great multitude. His eyes were fixed on the Rider in the distance ahead of him.

When all was over, and the Lord had dismounted, Joey took the donkey and her colt and led them away. He did not know where the Lord had gone when He dismounted, but His two followers had taken the donkey and her colt by the bridles and given them to Joey. He led them back, content with the wonderful thing that had happened and asking nothing more.

He brought Beckie and the colt to the stable, rubbed them down and brought their mash and water. Then he knelt down and kissed their hoofs because they had carried the Lord into Jerusalem. He put their rugs over them and went home.

Joey's brothers were there, talking excitedly.

"There are extraordinary rumors," they said. "People say that after His grand entry, the Prophet wept and said strange and terrible things about Jerusalem."

"Some say He will be arrested and put to death."

"But here's Joey. Come here, child, and tell us — " But the young man's words died on his lips. All three brothers stood open-mouthed, staring at Joey. And then the eldest of them said, "How ever did you come by that coat?"

Joey looked down. He lifted his arm and looked at his sleeve. Was it really his coat, or had he picked up another boy's by mistake? But there on the hem was the patch Mother had put on last week, and there at the elbow was her neat piece of darning. Yet it was a different coat, a coat embroidered or stamped all over with a strange, beautiful pattern of glowing blues and scarlets, and running through it all were threads of gold. He looked closer and he saw that the pattern was

made by the shape of the colt's hoofs and of the leaves and little branches the people had strewn before the Lord. But in each half-moon curve of the hoofs, there were grapes, ears of wheat, crimson thorns, and shapes like nails. He answered his brothers in a whisper, "It *is* my old coat. I laid it on the ground for the Lord to pass over."

The older boys were silent for a long time, staring at the coat. Then at last one of them said softly, "He *is* the Messiah. He *is* the Son of God!"

Giving Mr. Oates

It was candy that first drew Kathleen to Mr. Oates. She was only six. Like Mr. Oates himself, she had a valiant spirit and was therefore not afraid of him, as some small children were. He was pleased at this, and Kathleen got to know him very well. Day after day she would slip away to Mr. Oates's store and sit on a sugar box while Mr. Oates told her stories. She always came home sucking bull's-eyes two at a time. Although she was glad when she went to school and began to get ready for her First Communion, she was sorry she could not visit Mr. Oates so often.

Mr. Oates's store was the only shop in Puddlecombe except for the Post Office and the small dry-goods store kept by the two Miss Minns, who sold tapes, buttons, and other such things that were beneath the notice of Mr. Oates. His shop stood by itself, fronting the sea on the cliff between the Catholic school and the residential part of Puddlecombe. On their way home from school, the children always stopped to look into the window of the store. It was full of very large glass bottles of bull's-eyes, round red Dutch cheeses, and whole sides of bacon. Everything was big, nothing small or trifling, in Mr. Oates's store, plentiful and satisfying even to look at.

Mr. Oates was big himself, very tall and very broad, with a head as round and cheeks as red as the Dutch cheeses. His hands were big, too, and his voice was booming and rather like a blustering wind. He was not in the least like anyone else in Puddlecombe.

For it was a very sleepy place. There was not even a cinema in it. It was not a country place or a village, but the suburb of a seaside town. The houses were all alike, and the people were all alike, too; all except Mr. Oates, who was as exciting as the others were dull. He did not behave like a grown-up person at all, but more like a very naughty boy whom nobody dared to put in the corner. If you told him something that teacher had said about behaving well, he would bang his mighty fist on the counter and roar, "Stuff and nonsense!" If you mentioned a punishment at home or at school, he would bellow, "Don't stand for it, I say. Show your mettle, rebel!" The Miss Minns said he was not *nice*. Colonel Cuddy said he was a Bolshevist, and the Vicar of Puddlecombe said he was an atheist. Father O'Reilly, the Catholic priest, did not say anything and was inclined to be rather friendly with him.

Actually, Mr. Oates was a "born Catholic," although no one knew this, not even Father O'Reilly. He had even made his first confession when he was nine, and he remembered it. But his father and mother had died, and his aunt had sent him to a Protestant school, and he had made up his mind that he didn't like religious people and didn't want any religion at all. But everyone agreed about Mr. Oates that, whatever his faults, he gave good measure of good food. If you bought a pound of apples, he threw one in for luck, and the children were certain of a handful of candy for nothing.

Kathleen had three special friends. She and her friends wanted very much to do something for the Faith, something big and with all the strength they could put into it! The four were Nancy, Peter, Kathleen, and Kathleen's brother Eric. After Kathleen herself, the other three were Mr. Oates's greatest friends.

Of course, the first thing Kathleen did when she had been a few days at school was to tell Mr. Oates that she would soon be making her First Communion. Nancy had said not to: "If you do, he will only say something awful." But Kathleen could not keep such a happy secret from her friend. He had told her a lot of lovely things about birds and mice, so she would tell him all about our Lord.

The result was just what Nancy had said. Mr. Oates rolled his eyes and stamped about the shop. "So they are going to make a goody-goody of you," he shouted at last. "The next thing they will be telling you is that Oates is not fit for you to know; that's what they'll tell you."

"But Mr. Oates," said Kathleen with her lips trembling, "I *would* know you. I'd rather die than not know you."

Mr. Oates shook his head. "Done for," he said. "That's what you'll be, done for, for good!"

As the feast of Corpus Christi came closer, Sister Monica began telling the first communicants to think of themselves as a present they were going to give to Jesus. "He gives Himself to you, and you will give yourselves to Him," she said.

The next day, the four had a meeting by themselves. "You know," said Kathleen to Eric, "I'd rather give Mr. Oates instead of myself as a present to Jesus. He is much bigger than I, and I know *I* like big presents."

"Silly," said Eric, "as if God minds whether a person's big or little."

"But He might like big *presents*," said Kathleen stubbornly.

"People like to give the sort of presents they like to get," put in Peter.

Kathleen was really trying to explain something holy in her heart, but Eric and Peter made it seem silly. But she stuck to her point. "Well, if I *do* give presents I like, I'll give Mr. Oates, 'cause I like him, and I don't like me so much."

"*Say*," said Nancy suddenly, "we might try it!"

"Try what, silly?" said Peter.

"Try giving Mr. Oates to God!"

"How on earth?" said Eric. "Why, you talk as if he were a daffodil that we could put in a vase on the altar!"

"No, I don't, but we could pray for his conversion. Father O'Reilly said he's not so bad as some people make out."

"But how could we do it?" said Peter. "We'd need perfect faith to move a mountain like him!"

Nancy leaned forward to Eric and whispered, "Kathleen's *got* perfect faith!" Eric blushed, but with pride and joy. Although he always teased Kathleen, he was very proud of her really and was terribly glad she was his sister.

"Right!" he said. "We will give Mr. Oates to God. Now then, what sacrifices shall we make?"

"I'm afraid," said Peter, who was the greediest of them all, "it will have to be candy. No candy until he is converted."

"Oh! But suppose he *never* is," gasped Nancy, who was very fond of candy, too.

"But he *will* be," said Kathleen. So it was decided.

It must have been the Devil who, knowing what the four had planned, put it into the minds of the Miss Minns, just at this time, to start selling candy. The dear old ladies really thought it would do good "and keep those innocent children out of Oates's store." To make their candy pleasing to parents as well as to children, they had it neatly done up in little packs of colored paper, tied with ribbon, and advertised that it was made only from the purest sugar.

Mr. Oates happened to pass the Minns' shop on the very day the notice first appeared. He gave a shout of scornful laughter. "Pure!" he bellowed. "Well, I'm blowed! I suppose *my* candy isn't pure. Oh, no! Good old peppermint sticks, honey drops, pear drops, sugar apples, full measure, value for money! Impure, are they? Look at the pure candy that dare not show its face, all wrapped up to keep itself clean. Bah!"

He shook his fist at the window, then strode on to his store. There he got down his bottles and took out a handful from each and laid them in four piles on the counter. "I *give* my candy to the kids," he said and chuckled.

At ten past four, Kathleen, Eric, Peter, and Nancy came along. Mr. Oates beamed. "Come right in," he said. Then, casually waving his hand to the counter, he added, "And help yourselves."

There was a sudden awkward silence. "No, thank you, Mr. Oates," said Kathleen.

BUTTER SCOTCH
TOFFIES
BISCUITS

And the three others, wishing they had spoken first, said, "No, thank you, Mr. Oates" in chorus.

"Well, bless my soul! What's up?"

"Oh, nothing."

"Nothing!" Mr. Oates suddenly began to go red. He got redder and redder until the veins swelled in his forehead and his eyes grew bigger and bigger. "I know!" he said at last. "You despise my candy. You prefer the Minns's miseries."

From that day, the battle began. The Miss Minns, who had laid in a large supply of candy, put notices everywhere in Puddlecombe to say, "Candy is now for sale at Minns Sisters. Only the purest sugar, and done up in hygienic packages."

Mr. Oates, determined to go down fighting or win, took up the challenge. "They *shall* eat my candy," he said. Everything was taken out of the windows of the store, and it was filled with huge bottles of candy: pear drops of immense size, green, orange, yellow, and red; large peppermint sticks, glossy and striped; golden slabs of butterscotch; and every possible "mixture." Not content with this, Mr. Oates began posting his own bills and sticking them on top of the Miss Minns's: "Candy. Decent, old-fashioned candy, impure and dyed with poison! Come to Oates's store, and see if you perish!"

The sight of Mr. Oates's newly arranged window was too much for the four children. "I can't pass that shop and keep my resolution," said Peter.

"Nor I," said Eric. So they had to avoid Mr. Oates's store altogether. Instead of going home that way, they went by the lower road around the cliff. But wherever they went, they saw notices: "Candy, candy, candy." So Mr. Oates was always alone now. He felt sure that the grown-ups had made the children think he was wicked, and he was terribly unhappy.

On a rather cold spring day, Father O'Reilly was walking wearily round Puddlecombe, visiting his flock, when he looked up and saw the candy-laden window of Mr. Oates's store. "Poor old Oates," he said aloud. "I think I'll step in and have a chat. No harm done." He knew nothing of the great candy battle raging in Puddlecombe, and he walked in expecting the usual gruff bellows with which Mr. Oates greeted all clergymen.

Mr. Oates was engaged at the back of his shop making an enormous brew of toffee. What a glad sight on this cold morning was his red face, glowing in the embers that boiled his cauldron! Father O'Reilly drew near. "Good day to you, Mr. Oates. This is a grand idea! Toffee apples. They do remind me of being a child."

Mr. Oates gulped. His face, though red, was quiet and sad. "I make them for the kids," he mumbled, "but I'm not good enough. They won't come near me."

"What! I can hardly believe it!"

"They used to. Every day the kids sat in this shop eating my candy. But now day after day passes, and I don't set eyes on them. It began with 'No, thank you, Mr. Oates,' and then they don't come at all." Really it was Kathleen and the others, Mr. Oates's best friends, and not *all* the Puddlecombe children that he was thinking of.

"Well, well," said Father O'Reilly, "there must be some *reason*, although I don't know what it can be. May I have a toffee apple?"

Mr. Oates cheered up. He was grateful that anyone wanted one of his apples. "Yes. And no, thank you, Your Reverence; I don't take money from the clergy. You're welcome."

No one knows just what they talked about. But the whole of Puddlecombe soon knew that Father O'Reilly and Mr. Oates had been eating sugar apples together in Mr. Oates's store, because the whole of Puddlecombe always knew anything unusual that happened within its borders.

That evening Father O'Reilly questioned the children, and it all came out. "You meant well, very well," said Father O'Reilly, "but you have made poor Mr. Oates quite miserable. He thinks you turned up your noses at him and his candy. Now you'd better go along and explain it to him."

The four felt sad and ashamed as they crept into Mr. Oates's store. It seemed to be all such a failure, all the prayer and sacrifices. They simply felt foolish. And Mr. Oates looked shy, too.

Eric had agreed to tell him. He leaned on the counter and fiddled with the weighing weights. "We do like you," he began.

Mr. Oates was silent.

"I *love* you," said Kathleen.

Mr. Oates was still silent.

"But, you see, we wanted to give you to God for a present for Kathleen's First Communion," explained Eric.

Mr. Oates looked astonished. "Give me to God? For a present!"

"Yes. You see, Kathleen wanted to give a *big* present. She thinks she is so small. So we all said we'd help by making sacrifices."

"Sacrifices! Sheep and oxen?" exclaimed Mr. Oates in a state of great bewilderment.

"No, but we gave up eating candy until you're converted, that's all."

"*All!*" said Mr. Oates, and whistled softly. "You did that for me?

"Well, for God really. But as we like you, and as Kathleen likes you awfully, we thought God would like you, too."

"It's fearfully hard," said Nancy, "because we do love your candy terribly, and we want it very much. But we won't give in, so we had to keep away from the store."

Mr. Oates was staring down at the counter. When he spoke, his voice was very gruff indeed. "When can you eat candy again?"

"When you are converted."

Slowly Mr. Oates went to the back of the shop and returned with four toffee apples. He put them down on the counter. "You can eat them *now*," he said.

The White Mouse's Story

I have always been tame, and I have always loved Timothy, to whom I belong. He has been to me, and is, like God is to you. I depend on him for my food, crumbs and bits of cheese. When I am in his hand, I am safer than anywhere else, for although he could kill me, even by squeezing me too tightly out of affection, the love he has for me makes him gentle. I know something about God, because, first of all, it is He who makes me do all I can to keep alive. I am not able to use my reason, as I have none, but I have instincts, which is God thinking for me and making me do things.

And second, the story of Bethlehem has been handed down from mouse to mouse through the ages, because, of course, some of our ancestors were in the stable and were among the first living things to look on the Christ Child.

I have had only one real adventure in my life, and that was terrible. There were parts of it I did not understand, as I believe is the case even with you, when an adventure is worth having.

When Timothy was fourteen, he left school and got a job delivering newspapers. I always went with him, in his pocket. It was a very pleasant room for me, with crumbs and dust in the corner, and sometimes string and odd pieces of barley sugar. Of course, I never looked out while we were on duty, for I am a well-trained mouse, and I know my place. I just sat in the pocket and listened to the talk, which was often interesting.

At one house, the cook always asked Timothy in for a cup of tea. She used to say, "Now *creep*, for if *she* hears you, she'll be wild. She can't stand boys, she's that bitter." I didn't know who *she* was, but judged her to be very unlike barley sugar and not at all nice.

"You know," the cook told Timothy, "she has had a bagful of trouble in her day, and she doesn't believe in the good God. She thinks it's God's fault that things haven't gone her own way. You just ought to pray for her, for she won't last many years and she isn't ready to face her Maker by a long way."

Another day she told us more: "You must not let her see you, Tim, for you'd remind her of her boy. You are like his photo; he grew up and went to war, and then he was 'missing.' That means he might have been killed or taken prisoner, but anyhow they never knew. There were times when the priest used to come and tell her God loves more than father or mother and He would take care of her boy and do the best for him, but she wouldn't listen. She wouldn't take any interest in what anyone said, and now she's old and sour, and she doesn't love anyone."

I know Tim worried, for we went to church for visits a lot, and I knew it was to pray for old Mrs. Sour, as we called her.

I tried to explain to Tim that anyone who doesn't love anyone else cannot understand God at all. Even I, mouse though I am, have learned through love. When I had five little mice of my own, I used my body to warm them, and all I ever did was done to keep them safe and snug.

I know, too, that when Tim is gentle to me and feeds me, it is because, as I've heard him say at catechism, he is made in the image and likeness of God. It is the likeness to God in him that makes him be so nice to something small like me.

I tried to tell him, but of course I can only squeak. But he got the idea somehow, and I had to suffer for it. But then Tim did, too.

"Look here, Minnie," he said to me, "I've got to save old Mrs. Sour's soul. I've got to make her feel like God feels to us; then she'll know her son is OK. I can't give her anything but you, to do the trick. She'll *have* to feed you and make you a warm nest, and she couldn't *help* wanting you and loving you."

He made holes in a cardboard box and put me into it. I can't tell you my terror! But Tim is the sort who never lets a decent thought die in him, so I lay still, shivering, and made no sound. He wrote a letter and put it on the box, and next day left me with the newspaper, addressed to Mrs. Sour. Cook was busy, and she hardly glanced at the box. She just took me up on the morning tea tray and left me. Mrs. Sour heaved about in bed a bit, and then sat up and saw the box. "What!" she said. "A parcel for me — how unusual!" And she opened the letter.

"Dear Mrs. Sour," it said, "I am sending you what I love more than anything. It is the only way for you to find out that God loves humans more than they love each other. You will feel like He does to us, when Minnie asks for food and a nest and all that. Hoping you will be saved in time. With love from Tim."

She did not seem pleased with the letter, although I thought it very beautiful, and I knew what a lot of copies Tim had made. But after a few grunts, she cut the string. I ran out at once, as I had been cramped in the box, and I ran up her arm under her woolly jacket. To my horror, she let out a bloodcurdling scream and knocked all the morning tea tray onto the floor. Scream after scream she gave, and I dashed from her arm, down the bed, into a corner, and up the curtain.

Cook came running in, followed by two other maids, and they stood around Mrs. Sour, fanning her with the dishcloths and dusters they had in their hands. When she could speak, she said, "A mouse, a mouse!" and to hear her tone of voice, you would have thought I was a lion.

Then she said, "I have been affronted," and showed Tim's letter to Cook. The letter had a funny effect on Cook, too. First she rocked with laughter, which made Mrs. Sour scarlet with fury; then she suddenly stopped laughing and wiped her eyes with her apron. I never saw so much hysteria in my life, but I am not often with ladies.

I took the chance of getting higher up and hiding in the fold of a curtain.

They started a search for me, and I felt sure they meant to do me harm. They poked about behind everything with brooms and brushes, but if I as much as put my head out from the fold of the curtain, they fell back screaming. I heard the word *cat* several times, and my heart beat all over my body.

At last I was able to slip down and hide in a dark place behind the wardrobe, and after what seemed hours, they went away, and Mrs. Sour was alone.

The day was all misery. I went flitting from place to place, and never a crumb came my way. My nest was destroyed and not a mouse-hole was there in the house. In any case, brown mice are my enemies. About four o'clock, I was in the drawing room and Mrs. Sour, who had become calm, was engaged in reading some old letters in a box. She laid them out on her knee one by one, and she cried over them. I hoped to nibble the edge of one when she put them down, and, bold with hunger, I crept right under her chair.

She read a letter in a loud whisper: "May I bring home my mouse?" it said. "She is very tame, and I do love her. I could not leave her at school. No one would feed her, and she would pine, and she would die." Another said, "Father O'Flynn says we can have white mice, because it shows us how God loves us, because when we look after them, we are looking after what depends on us."

Mrs. Sour sat for a long time reading the letters. Then she put a bit of sugar and a little saucer of milk on the edge of the table and kept very still; and I grew bold, for I knew what had happened. I crept out and began to nibble. Then she put her old hand out, and I crept into it. It was not like Tim's, warm and soft, but cold and stiff, and I felt fear in it. But I stayed there, and very slowly, as if it hurt, she curled her fingers gently around me. Presently she carried me to her room, and a nightlight was brought and beside it I was given a box of cotton wool. And twice in the night the old lady brought me some bread and milk.

It was a better night than I had expected, although Mrs. Sour and I were not really at our ease together; and I was very relieved when Tim came into the room with Cook in the morning. I rushed to him and buried myself in his pocket. I didn't listen to their talk at first. I was faint with joy. When I came around, Mrs. Sour was saying, "Yes, I do see. If it is God who makes us feel that way even to mice when they depend on us, He *must* care for my boy, and *His* boy."

Tim nodded and said, "And if I would give Minnie to you and trust *you*, you ought to let God have your boy and not be sour over it!"

"That's all right," said Mrs. Sour. "I have said my prayers last night; but *please* take your mouse away. If only God would give back my boy the same way!"

"But that's just what He *will* do, if you save your soul and go to Heaven," said Tim.

We went away very happy. We visit Mrs. Sour sometimes. She has lots of Tim's friends to tea, too, other boys, but I am kept in his pocket and never look out. But I get plenty of cake crumbs at those teas, and Tim says I saved the old woman's soul.

Anna Kluyer

Anna Kluyer knelt before the icon, and she felt that there was no one in Rumania more to be pitied than herself. And although Anna had run out of her home in a tantrum, leaving the three little ones without their supper and with no one to see them to bed, and although she had grieved her good father sorely with the things she had said to him, our Lady looked kindly upon Anna; for she, too, had once been a little peasant girl, fourteen years old, with great responsibility resting on her.

But in the icon, our Lady was not shown as a peasant, but as a queen. She was clothed richly in a gown of crimson, her slender throat clasped in a collar of pearls, and a veil as white as snow swathed across her brow and around the dark sweet oval of her face. She was crowned with a heavy golden crown that flamed with emeralds. In the crook of her arm, the divine Child was seated, and He, too, was shown royally, vested in a thick cope of golden brocade, His thin little face seeming very tiny under its crown and ringed with a halo encrusted thickly with jewels.

Anna told her sad story, kneeling with her eyes closed. "After all, I asked for so little, just a red gown like yours, a red silk dress to wear in the procession. They need not have laughed, my father and the children. They need not have said, 'What! A peasant girl! Do you think you are a queen?' And if we are so poor that I cannot have a silk dress, why has my father brought home Afanasy for us to bring up? Have I not had enough to do bringing up Lubov and Yakov? And now that they are seven years old and go to school, my father brings home Afanasy, who is only three, and tells me to love him as if he were my brother! If he has money enough to adopt Afanasy, could he not give me pretty dresses and perhaps a little maid to help in the kitchen?"

She looked up at the Blessed Mother, but the dark, tender face looked gravely on her, and the divine Child looked with sad, unsmiling eyes. "O holy Mother, do not be angry," said Anna, and she burst into tears. "I want to be as you are. Just for a little while," she sobbed. "I am tired of cooking and washing and mending and of little Afanasy. If I could be a queen in a red gown and a crown of gold and carry the little King in the crook of my arm, just for one hour . . ."

The Blessed Mother bowed her head slowly under its weight of gold and, lifting her long thin hand from the holy Child, beckoned to Anna.

* * *

Everything seemed very strange at first. Anna was afraid. She was so high up, and the church looked odd and new seen from above. She could not turn her head in the stiff collar of pearls, and the crown was heavy. She could not move her eyes to look at the holy Child, who made her arm ache sitting in the crook of it with all his heavy ornaments. She had to look straight down at the people who came in and out of church, just as the icon was painted to look down.

She could see the candle flames that were at her feet. They were like a pool of light that rippled with golden waves, and beyond them was darkness. Only now and again she heard the door of the church opening and saw a slit of blue beyond the gold. Then it would swing heavily back, and a peasant's face would be lifted up among the flames, and the familiar voice of a neighbor would speak to her from down below.

Some came in to thank the dear Mother for a good day's work without sorrow or sickness coming to mar it; and Anna felt ashamed because she had never thought to bless the Queen of Heaven for her own strength to work. Some bowed very low so that she saw only the tops of their heads, and they asked pardon for their sins; and Anna blushed scarlet behind the candles because it had always been other people's sins that she had spoken of in her prayers.

Presently, when the church had been empty for a long while, she heard the sound of children's feet tiptoeing in, and lifted among the lights she saw the round, dirty faces of her little brother and sister, Lubov and Yakov. How dirty they looked to come before the Queen of Heaven! Lubov's hair was rough and tangled, and her eyes were red from crying. Yakov had grazed his chin, and his cheek was smeared with dirt.

Anna tried to stretch out her hand to them, but she could not move it. She could only remain quite still, just as the icon was painted, and listen to their prayers.

Lubov whispered, "Please, darling Mother, send Anna back. She went out in a temper because Papa can't afford to give her a silk dress, and we laughed. I have brought my string of green beads that Papa gave to me. I was going to give it to Anna because she can't have the dress, but I will give it to you if you will send her back."

Then, thin and shaky through the sighing of the flames, came the little boy Yakov's voice: "Holy Mother, do send her. We haven't had our supper. And we don't know how to undress Afanasy, so we've put him to bed in his clothes, but he won't stop crying for his milk, and the milk is on the high shelf, and we can't reach it, and Papa isn't home yet. I brought you half a sugar stick for an offering to bring Anna back. I didn't *mean* to eat half on the way, but I was hungry."

"I licked it, too. I am sorry," said Lubov's voice.

Yakov went on, "But it isn't only our supper we want; it's Anna," and he began to cry.

Then the voices stopped, and Anna saw the two dark heads close together and knew that the children were whispering. She could catch a word here and there: "I think we could. You see, our Lady must *know* already. It wouldn't be telling tales. . . . Well, you say it. . . ."

Lubov stood a little forward and said timidly, "Please, our Lady, when you send Anna back, could she be not so cross always?" Then the two dirty small children padded out of church.

Anna longed to follow them. It was very stiff and cold up in the icon frame. The jeweled Infant was far heavier than little Afanasy. She thought of them hungry and dirty at home and Afanasy in bed in his clothes, the milk out of their reach. She knew that at least an hour would pass before her father went home. Suppose, she thought, they try to light the lamp and catch fire! But Anna could not move from the icon frame.

The door of the church opened again, and her father came in. He looked troubled, but she knew that he had not yet been home and found her missing. He had something small and dark in his hand. He bowed very solemnly to the icon seven times. Then he spoke: "Most holy Mother of God, guide me, poor foolish Vladimir Kluyer, your servant. I am in darkness. Send the light of your wisdom. My little girl Anna has looked after my home since her mother died and cared for my babies, Lubov and Yakov.

"She could not do it very well, but I have been patient because she was young, and when the soup was all salt, I said, no word, or when the kitchen was dirty and my clothes unmended, I did not complain. For I said, 'She is so young, and she does her best, and she loves me as I love her. Love will make excuses. Love will make our little family content.' Even when she scolds the little ones too much, I am silent, for I say, 'She will learn to be patient in time, and they will become easier as they grow.'

"But two months ago, my neighbor Marinka, who had been a widow, died, leaving her baby, Afanasy, an orphan. And for the love of your little Son, Jesus, I took him home to be our own. Now Anna is angry, because we must sacrifice much for this little stranger, and she wants fine dresses. Should I send away the baby for Anna's sake?"

The good man looked up, and Anna saw how tired he was, but he went on: "I mean to give her a silk dress after all. She is young, and all young people want pretty things. It is for me to make a sacrifice: I will not spend my money anymore on smoking. I have brought my pipe, dear Mother. It has been my best friend, but I would like to keep Afanasy, because I love him for your little Son's sake."

And at the foot of the icon Vladimir Kluyer laid his old black pipe that was the comfort of his long evenings alone. He turned and went out.

Anna would have wept, but the painter had painted no tears on the face of God's Mother, so she could only look down, clear-eyed, at the three things that lay at her feet: a string of glass beads, half of a red sugar stick, and an old polished pipe.

She looked at those things, wondering, for they were signs of the love that had always

been given to her and that she had never even thought of.

After a time, the door opened again, and this time her father was carrying Afanasy in his arms and Lubov and Yakov were crying lustily on each side of him. "Hush now," said the poor father. "Do not cry so. Our Lady will send her back, and you have had your supper now."

"It isn't supper," wailed Lubov and Yakov. "It's Anna we want. O holy Mother, send her back even if she is just as horrid and cross as before. We want Anna!"

Then Vladimir Kluyer made little Afanasy cross himself, guiding his small hand in his big one, and holding him up to Anna, he said, "Holy Mother, you cannot say no to the little one whom I have treated as your own Son. Send naughty Anna home to us!"

Anna looked at Afanasy, and she saw that his face was just the face of the divine Child in the icon, only it was uncrowned and alive. And she longed to lift her hands from the jeweled painted Baby, who was only a picture, and to go down to the little living one who, needing her, was truly Jesus to her. She wanted to go home and sweep and wash and bake and to kiss the too-much-scolded twins and dance Afanasy on her knees.

When at last the hour she had prayed for was over, Anna stepped down through the lights and flowers and found herself again at our Lady's feet. She picked up the pipe and the beads and the sugar stick and turned to our Lady. "Thank you," she said. "Thank you, dear Mother, for showing me. Now I will show them that I, too, can love. I thought I would be happy if I were a queen, but I know now how I will be happy."

Anna ran home. She was there before the little family, there in time to clear away the children's supper and set her father's. She spread a clean white cloth and brought out a new loaf of bread. She poured his beer into a shining tankard and set his pipe by his plate. Then she tidied the room and awaited their coming.

Petook

It was a lovely warm day. The sky was bright blue and the clouds white and thick, like balls of cotton wool. Everything seemed full of color — big, happy colors like those in a painting book. Even the maize in the bowls was yellower than usual.

Petook was happy. He had reason to be: he was a fine cock with snowy-white plumage and a red comb that positively glowed in the sun, and today he had become the father of twelve little chickens. He thought that there were no chickens like them, none so round, so yellow, so fluffy, so bright-eyed. As for his wife, Martha, the brown speckled hen, plain and homely soul though she was, she had become all grand and important.

During the past weeks, Petook had sometimes felt a little impatient. It seemed that Martha had some secret that he did not share. It made *her* very happy, but it also made her look almost *smug*, and it annoyed Petook to be outside of it. Martha had just sat on the eggs with a tiny smile on her face and her eyes nearly shut, as if she were looking into herself at a ball of light that was growing inside. Not talking, not moving, only making a funny little sound of happiness in her throat now and then. But now Petook understood. It was he who was smiling, and so bursting with pride and joy that he could not speak.

Petook was sitting on the wooden gatepost dreaming of his family when a group of hens ran up to him.

"Come!" they clucked. "Some stranger has been walking through the vineyard."

Petook, who was as inquisitive as any hen, although he would not have liked it to be known, got up at once and hurried off with the others.

Sure enough, there on the dewy grass beneath the vines were the impressions of a child's feet. They were set in a straight line toward Jerusalem. But Petook knew that between the vine and road to Jerusalem was the chicken run, and Martha and the children. He began to fly, in short, violent bursts of flight, back to his family. All the way he was saying to himself, "I am sure that they were a boy's footsteps and boys are sometimes careless, even when they're not cruel. He might tread on one of the chicks." Petook could see that some of the fruit fallen under the vines *had* been trodden and crushed.

When he got to Martha, he knew that he need not have been afraid. It is true that there was a boy there, but this Boy was kneeling by the little brown hen with a look of wonder on his face, quite spellbound by the lovely sight of Martha gathering the chicks under her wings. His hands, which were thin and golden, were spread out like protecting wings over Martha. His lips were slightly parted, his eyes shining. So rapt was he that Petook thought, "It must be the first time he has seen a hen gathering her chickens." For Martha, prouder than ever, was ducking softly and pushing the little ones in under her wings.

Petook preened himself. He strutted up and down, and round and round. He noticed every detail of the day, just as people notice every detail in a picture if it is rare and lovely, and one that they may not see again. He noticed how strong-looking the slim hands were, that the Child's garment was woven without a seam, and that the sandaled feet were stained with the splashes of juice by treading on fruit fallen from the vine. Suddenly, for sheer joy, Petook lifted his head and crowed.

* * *

Years had gone by. Petook was quite old. He had just passed through an uneasy night. Everything had been steeped in moonlight, but all had looked strange and sad. He could see the distant hill of Calvary where three tall tree trunks always stood. Only when someone was to die did they become crosses, for then the poor person brought the beam that was fastened across for him to hang on. By getting on top of the dovecote and stretching his neck, Petook could just see the crosses as dark bars on the shining sky. It seemed as if morning would never come. Martha was puffed out, sleeping on her eggs, and there was no one to talk to. The moonlight made long black shadows on the grass, and the grass was like pale green water. But suddenly there came a break in the sky and, like a red wound, morning came. And suddenly Petook crowed out loud and long, for he felt somehow excited and lifted up, he could not tell why.

All day long, he kept returning to the dovecote and looking, as if a spell were on him, at the crosses. At about midday, or maybe a little after, Petook saw that there was a little smudge at the top of the hill, which must be people. And then the crossbeam went up. When he saw it, he slowly opened his wings, for to him the cross looked just like that, like the opening of great wings. Of course, he did not know who was being lifted up there. He did not know that it was the lovely little Boy, or that the little Boy had remembered Martha and her chicks years after and had said to hardhearted men: "Jerusalem, Jerusalem, how often would I have gathered you under my wings as the hen gathers her chicks, and you would not."

It was three days later, a morning cloaked with sunlight as with a garment of golden gossamer. Petook's dark mood had changed. He had a feeling of certainty that Martha's chicks would come out of the eggs today. It would be dawn in a few minutes, and the chicks would come. He felt sure of it.

There was a soft step on the grass. It was the farmer's wife. She loved the fowls, and they trusted her. Now she knelt down by Martha, and Martha did not open her eyes, but made a soft gurgle of greeting in her throat. The woman put her hand gently under the hen's breast and drew out an egg. It was a lovely egg, a soft golden-pink color, and it lay in the palm of the kind hand, warm and beautiful. The woman put the egg back.

Then she leaned down; she was listening. Petook was listening, too. So were the blades of grass, and the drops of dew on them; so were the leaves on the trees, and the stars that lingered still in the sky. The world was listening. Petook knew that. The trees everywhere were listening. All the winds held their breath. Every flower and leaf and bird was still. It was so quiet that Petook heard the chickens in the eggs tapping softly with their beaks to get out.

Yes, Petook heard that, and he heard life everywhere, tapping softly, knocking softly to get out, to come out of the dark into the light, out of silence into sound, out of death into life: bird and beast and seed in the earth and bud on the tree. Petook heard all that when the chickens tapped to get out. And suddenly one of them came — a struggling splutter of gold fluff. The woman laughed, and the sky broke into a splendor of light.

Petook threw back his head and crowed and crowed and crowed. His red comb burned in glory, the white feathers in his plumage dazzled in the light, and the new chicken danced at his feet. He crowed again and again and again. It was Easter morning.

Biographical Note

Caryll Houselander

Frances Caryll Houselander was born in Bath, England, in 1901. Caryll, as she is known, and her sister were baptized into the Catholic Church in 1907. Her parents separated when she was nine years old. She was then sent to convent schools until she was sixteen.

Personal troubles caused her to leave the Catholic Church for a while. During these years, she went to St. John's Wood Art School in London. She worked at many jobs and tried other religions.

In her twenties, she returned to the Catholic Church. She worked for the Church as a painter and woodcarver.

Caryll Houselander wrote articles and drew pictures for *The Children's Messenger*. She also wrote articles for *The Grail Magazine*. Some of these were printed in her first book, *This War Is the Passion*, which was published in 1941, during World War II. She also drew the illustrations for the children's book *My Path to Heaven*, written by Geoffrey Bliss.

Caryll Houselander wrote many books in her lifetime. *A Rocking-Horse Catholic* tells the story of her childhood and youth. Many have read her book *The Reed of God*, which is about the Virgin Mary.

Caryll Houselander saw the image of Jesus in all men, women, and children. She served the Catholic Church with joy. Her writings have helped many Christians to love Jesus more and to become more like Him. She died in 1954.

Sophia Institute Press®

Sophia Institute® is a nonprofit institution that seeks to restore man's knowledge of eternal truth, including man's knowledge of his own nature, his relation to other persons, and his relation to God. Sophia Institute Press® serves this end in numerous ways: it publishes translations of foreign works to make them accessible to English-speaking readers; it brings out-of-print books back into print; and it publishes important new books that fulfill the ideals of Sophia Institute®. These books afford readers a rich source of the enduring wisdom of mankind.

Sophia Institute Press® makes these high-quality books available to the general public by using advanced technology and by soliciting donations to subsidize its general publishing costs. Your generosity can help Sophia Institute Press® to provide the public with editions of works containing the enduring wisdom of the ages. Please send your tax-deductible contribution to the address below. We also welcome your questions, comments, and suggestions.

For your free catalog, call:

Toll-free: 1-800-888-9344

or write:

Sophia Institute Press®

Box 5284, Manchester, NH 03108

or visit our website:

www.sophiainstitute.com

Sophia Institute® is a tax-exempt institution
as defined by the Internal Revenue Code,
Section 501(c)(3). Tax I.D. 22-2548708.